DUSTY & OLD HARRY

Issue 1
First Published in 2022

Author
George Wellesley Pritchard

Illustrator
Vicki Noble

Cover Design
Celia J-Hale

This book is produced for sale in order in order to raise funds for the erection of a National Monument for the RAF crews of the Photo Reconnaissance Unit that were lost in World War II.

This Unit had a casualty rate of fifty percent. Many bodies were never found and their graves are where they fell. Some were killed if captured on Hitler's orders. Your donation will be greatly appreciated.

www.spitfireaa810.co.uk

IT was a lovely spring day as Jane looked out of the window at the garden and the sky. Birds were singing and flocking to the birdbath. Spring flowers were beginning to make their entrance, breaking through the warm brown earth.

"Oh Dusty!" said Jane, running into the bedroom. "It is such a lovely day, we should go out. Let's go and pay a visit to my elderly great aunt in the country. It's quite a long way so mummy is taking us in the car. It will be a wonderful trip out. I call her aunt Tilly, even though she's my great aunt, so you can call her that too, Dusty"

Jane got herself ready then picked up Dusty, her much loved teddy bear and carried him excitedly to the car.

She cuddled him tightly throughout the long journey to see her aunt. She was happily telling him stories about her aunt and some of the adventures she has had in the countryside whilst she was staying with her.

When they arrived, her aunt was so pleased to see them, chattering away as she showed her visitors into the dining room.

Jane's eyes bulged at the sight of the lovely table her aunt had laid for them with tea, sandwiches, scones and homemade cakes. Jane dutifully washed her hands, first carefully putting Dusty on a big armchair so that he could see the banquet they were about to enjoy.

Dusty took the opportunity to look around the room and discovered that he was sitting next to an old, much-loved teddy bear. This bear had almost no hair left on him; he looked as old as Jane's aunt Tilly.

"Hello," he said, "My name is Dusty." The old bear looked at him kindly, so Dusty continued to explain "I'm called Dusty because a long time ago I was carelessly dropped in the muddy road by the van driver when he was delivering me and other toys to Mr Trimble's toy shop. I'm not dusty now though as I was given a bath."

"Ho ho!" the old bear laughed gently. "Well I thought that was a funny name for a Teddy, but I do understand now, and it suits you, though you don't look dusty now. My name is Harry, I used to be called Hairy Harry, but I think that now I should be called hairless Harry." And he laughed at his own joke as he surveyed his new friend. "Is aunt Tilly your owner?" said Dusty.

"She is now, but I used to belong to her son, Peter, who bought me when he was four years old from the local toy shop. We had lots of fun together, he used to throw me high in the sky and then catch me, he never missed or let me fall but lots of my fur came off over the years with the rough games and adventures we had together."

Harry continued, "When Peter grew up, he called me his lucky mascot and said that I would always bring him good luck. We went everywhere together. In 1939, when he was eighteen, a terrible war began, and everyone had to go to war with people from another country.

These people were called the 'Nasties' I believe. Peter was a clever lad and went off to join the Air Force where he learnt to fly special aeroplanes which were used to take important photographs of these 'Nasties' in their country. They were called The Photo Reconnaissance Unit (PRU).

He took me with him during the war to the aerodrome, and to his room there. Before he went flying every day, he would always rub my fluffy ears because he said it gave him good luck. Then I had to just wait and hope my luck worked and he got back safely."

Dusty could see now why Harry had so little hair, especially on his ears, but it didn't detract from his wonderful personality at all. He was such a nice old bear, with a kindly face and a warm laugh.

Harry smiled at the young bear's interest in him, so he continued. "One day Peter decided to take me with him in his aeroplane. He sat me down at the front in a great position, where I could see everything that was going on around me. It was very exciting to be flying so high in the sky and looking down at the fields and towns. Soon we were flying over the sea, which looked grey and deep in the early dawn, and I hoped Peter would keep us safe up there in the sky.

We saw land once more and everything looked so tiny from up in the sky. It was then that Peter told me that I had to keep very still and quiet because he was going to take some very important photos of buildings and submarines. The aeroplane slowed and swooped, moving steadily as Peter concentrated on taking the photos. When he was finished taking photos we began to climb high into the sky once more and head back across the sea to our aerodrome".

Suddenly, Peter started to look a bit scared and made his plane fly up and down, higher then lower, to the right and the left. Even doing a big loop in the sky whilst behind us there was lots of noise coming from other aeroplanes in the sky.

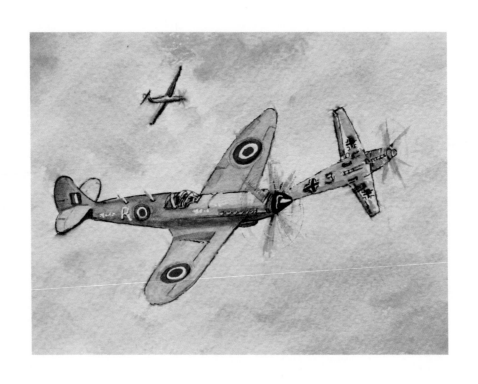

They were chasing us and the bangs and pops, when the Nasties fired their guns at us, were not nice at all. I was quite frightened and wondered why Peter didn't fire his guns too. But he told me that his plane didn't have any guns, it had cameras instead. Peter said that while I was with him, as his lucky mascot, we would be safe from anything bad happening to us.

He was right, of course, we were very safe and it wasn't long before we landed back at the aerodrome just in time for a well-deserved breakfast. "Wow!" said a wide-eyed Dusty, "You really did keep Peter safe and have some amazing adventures. I would love to fly."

Harry just smiled again. He was rather enjoying this. "So, every time Peter flew his Spitfire plane after that I went with him to keep him safe. No one minded at all because all the pilots had a lucky charm or mascot to help them keep safe.

After a few years the war stopped. There was no more fighting, everyone became friends, and we all went home to our families. Peter then met a lovely lady, got married and went away to live in another place with her. He left me here with his mother, Tilly, as he felt I would have a bit more peace and quiet here, away from his noisy children. Sometimes, he comes here to see his mother and always says hello to me, ruffling my ears fondly."

Thank you for telling me about your life and adventures, it was so very interesting. I would really like to meet Peter one day. You have been a very lucky bear indeed, a hero in fact. I do hope we can come back soon," said Dusty "And then I will be able to tell you about all of the adventures that I have been having with Jane. Dusty cuddled up to Old Harry and thanked him again in Teddy talk and Dusty showed Harry a high five!

"I hope that you will come again very soon too," said Harry. Time had passed quickly. Dusty saw that it was time for the ride back home, as Jane picked him up and after hugs and fond farewells and promises that they would be back soon, they left fo the long journey back home. "I think that you liked sitting with Harry," said Jane, "Auntie Tilly's cakes were delicious, and she is such a lovely auntie."

Dusty smiled contentedly as he and Jane drifted off to sleep together on the journey home, each of them dreaming of the day's adventures, of Jane chatting to auntie and Dusty hearing stories about some of the heroes during the war. What a day!

THE END

Written by
George Wellesley Pritchard
Illustrated by
Vicki Jane Noble

Printed in Great Britain
by Amazon

16609794R00025